Sid, Spark
and the
Signal Man

ORPEN PRESS

Acknowledgements

I would like to thank the Human Givens College for recognising and encouraging my creativity. I especially thank the college principal Ivan Tyrrell and Director of Studies Joe Griffin for their inspirational teaching of the most effective and transforming psychotherapy I have learned to date.

I also thank Brenda O'Hanlon, my editor, for believing in me, working so hard and doing such a wonderful job. I am sincerely grateful to Sue Saunders for sorting out the computer and being my right hand in Ireland. Without her IT expertise and patience these stories might not have reached the publisher so promptly!

Thank you to my colleague Sue Harper for listening to my first story and telling me to "go for it", and to Pat Williams, founder-director of the London College of Storytellers, for advising me to get the stories published. Thanks also to all my colleagues and friends who have encouraged me over the years.

Of course, most importantly, I thank my incredibly supportive husband Frank, who is my best friend and my stability, and who has allowed me to remain a child at heart.

And a big thank you to all the children who have inspired me, and without whom I would not have known the healing properties of these stories.

Sid, Spark
and the
Signal Man

Written by Pamela Woodford
Illustrations by Beatrice Cornes

ORPEN PRESS
Lonsdale House
Avoca Ave
Blackrock
Co. Dublin
Ireland

e-mail: info@orpenpress.com
www.orpenpress.com

© Pamela Woodford, 2013
ISBN: 978-1-871305-82-1

Printed in Northern Ireland by GPS Colour Graphics Ltd

Preface

STORIES HAVE ALWAYS BEEN a powerful way of conveying universal human dreams and dreads, of inspiring us to find strengths we didn't know we had, to overcome difficulties, and to flourish and grow.

Stories are particularly effective with children, as I know from my work as a consultant Human Givens psychotherapist over the past twelve years. During that time, I have told countless stories, many of which I made up myself, and I've found that the right story can get to the heart of the matter and bring about swift, positive change.

Children as young as five, but also adolescents and adults, have heard my stories, which have proved to be a key way of addressing imperative issues.

All the stories in the *Brighter Little Minds* series encourage the reader/listener to use their imagination in a positive way. There are also suggestions for activities that aim to further embed the learning and therapeutic metaphor contained in each book. The story of *Sid, Spark and the Signal Man* addresses such issues as: anger management, family problems, bullying, violence, learning self-control, learning rules, working together, developing empathy and much more.

Suggestions for Activities:

Make three flags in red, orange and green.

Working as a group or in pairs, help each other to decide which flags would be applicable for different scenarios.

Act out the scenarios with and without the use of the flags.

"Chuggedy-chuggedy, chuggedy-chuggedy, chuggedy-chuggedy, woo-oo, woo-oo!" That was a train named Sid.

"Chuggedy-chuggedy, chuggedy-chuggedy, chuggedy-chuggedy, woo-oo, woo-oo!" And that was a train named Spark.

Sid and Spark were travelling along on their railway tracks, side by side. Sid was an older and bigger train, and was painted in bright blue and yellow.

Spark was a younger, smaller train and was painted in lots of bright, bold colours that he had chosen for himself.

Both trains had to be sure to keep their engines in good working order. They were kept beautifully clean and were polished until they shone. Most days, Sid and Spark travelled alongside each other chatting happily: "Chuggedy-chuggedy, chuggedy-chuggedy, woo-oo, woo-oo!" That's the way that trains tell each other things – "Woo-oo, woo-oo!" Sid and Spark felt good when they told each other things.

Sometimes, the railway tracks needed to change direction, and the lines had to be properly controlled. And who better to do this than the signal man?

The signal man had his own little office, high above the railway line. It had big, clear windows that allowed him to see for miles around.

He would notice when trains weren't getting on well together and then decide the best course of action. The signal man loved his job. He took his lunch with him to work, plus his favourite drink in a little flask.

After all, it was hungry and thirsty work making sure that all the trains went safely and happily on their journeys.

The signal man used three flags, which worked very well together.

First, in order to prevent collisions or if he could see danger ahead, he would raise his **red flag** and wave it high in the air so that the trains could be warned to **stop immediately**.

Then there was an **orange flag** that he would wave if there were lots of other trains coming and he needed them to chuggedy-chug **a little slower**.

He also had a **green flag** which the signal man waved when **all was very well** and the trains could continue on their journeys.

The signal man was very good at his job. He always knew and remembered that it was a highly important task to keep the trains chuggedy-chugging along safely and happily side by side.

Sid was trying to teach Spark all about the signals, how they worked and how extremely important it was to take notice of them.

If the trains ignored the signals to slow down or to stop, then this could cause some real problems.

And so to help Spark learn, Sid told him a story about his great-great-grandfather, Albert, who had been a steam train.

Now, steam trains were built to use just the right amount of steam in order to keep them sh-sh-shussing on the tracks happily: sssshh-ssshh-sshh-shh, sssshh-ssshh-ssh-shh, sssshh-ssshh-sshh-shh, ssshh-ssshh-sshh-shh.

But Albert had a problem – he had a habit of letting off too much steam and had almost fallen apart because of it. He usually let off too much steam when he wanted to get his own way. His engine would become hotter and hotter, and then it would overheat to almost boiling point.

One day, when Albert was sh-sh-shussing along, he met another steam train named Wilfred, who was on another track.

They sh-sh-shussed alongside each other for quite a while. However, while Albert was thinking of what *he* wanted to do and where *he* wanted to go, Wilfred was also thinking about what *he* wanted to do and where *he* wanted to go.

This is where the problem seems to have started. Albert and Wilfred both wanted different things, and both were determined to get their own way. Neither of them gave any thought to the other. They just began to let off as much steam as possible and away they went!

They dug their wheels into the tracks as hard as they could. Sshh-sshh, sshh-sshh, sshh-sshh, sshh-sshh—faster and faster, faster and faster—sshh-sshh, sshh-sshh, sshh-sshh, sshh-sshh—faster and faster, faster and faster.

The faster they went, the more and more steam they let off. Their engines were getting hotter and hotter until they overheated and were suddenly brought to the boil! It's a wonder the trains didn't melt on the spot with all the heat they were making.

And now they were so lost in their own steam that they couldn't even see where they were going …

… so much so that they had totally missed the signal man's **orange flag** which had been telling them to **slow down** and then the signal man's **red flag**, which of course had been ordering them to **stop immediately!**

While all this was happening, the metal railway tracks had become so hot that sparks began to fly off in all directions.

This really caused such a scary scene: the Catherine wheels whizzed round and round, spinning out of control; the rockets took off and whooshed high in the air; and it seemed that all the fireworks were exploding at the same time.

All that screeching and screaming – what a frightening noise! Albert and Wilfred covered their ears, confused and wondering about what was going on. Oh, how they wished it would all come to an end!

Then, gradually, just as if their wishes had been magically granted, one by one all the sparks cooled down. They felt much more peaceful and happy when the noise faded away.

By this time, Albert and Wilfred had slowed their engines down until they had finally brought themselves to a halt. It was only then, as they settled, that their steam began to lift and they could see each other again. As they looked into each other's faces, they realised how silly and selfish they had been.

15

In fact, letting off all that steam hadn't actually got them anywhere.

Albert and Wilfred never let off too much steam again, and they always watched out for the signal man's flags.

"Wow," said Spark, who had been listening carefully to Sid's story. "If I was a steam train I would keep my engine in good working order, by not getting all het up and just staying cool."

"Well done," said Sid. And
then Spark began to laugh.

"What's so funny?" asked Sid.

"Well," Spark answered, "I
was just thinking that Albert
reminded me of a kettle
coming to the boil and
making lots of steam."

"And so," said Spark,
"every time I have a cup of
tea I will think about this
story, and I might even call
my kettle Albert!"

"Brilliant idea," said Sid. "Let's go and have a cup of tea together."

And as they did, Spark noticed the signal man who was waving his **green flag**, which meant that **all was very well** and they could continue on their journey.

Chuggedy-chuggedy, chuggedy-chuggedy, chuggedy-chuggedy, woo-oo, woo-oo!

THE END

Sid, Spark
and the
Signal Man